ONE WORLD WITH A SECRET IN THEIR

ASPEN UNIVERSE
REVELATIONS

ONE WORLD WITH A SECRET IN THEIR SEAS...

FATHOM & SOULFIRE CREATED BY:
MICHAEL TURNER

ASPEN UNIVERSE: REVELATIONS™ VOLUME 1
ISBN: 978-1-941511-25-1 FIRST PRINTING, REGULAR EDITION 2016.
COLLECTS MATERIAL ORIGINALLY PUBLISHED AS WORLDS OF ASPEN 2016 #1, ASPEN UNIVERSE: REVELATIONS VOL.1 1-5.

PUBLISHED BY ASPEN MLT, INC.
OFFICE OF PUBLICATION: 5701 W. SLAUSON AVE. SUITE. 120, CULVER CITY, CA 90230.

Address correspondence to:
ASPEN UNIVERSE c/o Aspen MLT Inc.
5701 W. Slauson Ave. Suite. 120
Culver City, CA. 90230-6946
or fanmail@aspencomics.com

Visit us on the web at:
aspencomics.com
aspenstore.com
facebook.com/aspencomics
twitter.com/aspencomics

ORIGINAL SERIES EDITORS:
VINCE HERNANDEZ AND FRANK MASTROMAURO

FOR THIS EDITION:
SUPERVISING EDITOR: FRANK MASTROMAURO
EDITOR: GABE CARRASCO
COVER DESIGN: MARK ROSLAN AND PETER STEIGERWALD
BOOK DESIGN AND PRODUCTION: MARK ROSLAN, PETER STEIGERWALD AND GABE CARRASCO
COVER ILLUSTRATION: JORDAN GUNDERSON AND PETER STEIGERWALD
ASPENSTORE.COM COVER ILLUSTRATION: JORDAN GUNDERSON AND PETER STEIGERWALD

FOR ASPEN:
FOUNDER: MICHAEL TURNER
CO-OWNER: PETER STEIGERWALD
CO-OWNER/PRESIDENT: FRANK MASTROMAURO
VICE PRESIDENT/EDITOR IN CHIEF: VINCE HERNANDEZ
VICE PRESIDENT/DESIGN AND PRODUCTION: MARK ROSLAN
EDITORIAL ASSISTANT: GABE CARRASCO
OFFICE COORDINATOR: MEGAN MADRIGAL
ASPENSTORE.COM: CHRIS RUPP

To find the
Comic Shop
nearest you...

888-COMIC-BOOK
csls.diamondcomics.co
1-888-266-4226

DIRECT EDITION COVER A TO
WORLDS OF ASPEN 2016 #1
BY
JORDAN **GUNDERSON** | PETER **STEIGERWALD**

PEN UNIVERSE
RELATIONS

Joshua Hale **FIALKOV**
& J.T. **KRUL**

SCRIPT

Jordan **GUNDERSON**
& Giuseppe CAFARO

PENCILS

Mark **ROSLAN**
Gabe CARRASCO & John ERCEK

DIGITAL INKS

Peter **STEIGERWALD**
& John STARR

COLORS

Josh **REED**

LETTERING

THERE ARE TWO DAYS IN MY LIFE THAT STAND OUT TO ME. TWO DAYS WHERE EVERYTHING CHANGED.

THE DAY I LEARNED I WASN'T HUMAN. THAT I WAS PART OF A SECRET WORLD ON THE OCEAN FLOOR.

OF THE BLUE AND THE BLACK.

THE SECOND DAY?

WHEN THERE STOPPED BEING TWO WORLDS, LEAVING BARELY ONE.

THE DAY
EVERYTHING
DRIED UP.

FORGET COAL. FORGET OIL.
WATER--THAT'S THE ULTIMATE
RESOURCE ON THE PLANET.
WITHOUT IT, EVERYTHING DIES.

PEOPLE THOUGHT THEY COULD
AVERT DISASTER WITH BABY
STEPS--DROUGHT RESISTANT
LAWNS, FIVE MINUTE SHOWERS,
FILLING IN SWIMMING POOLS.

WHEN THE DUST BOWL STARTED AGAIN
IN OKLAHOMA. THAT OPENED THEIR EYES. IT
SPREAD TO TEXAS, KANSAS, MISSOURI. ONCE IT
HIT LOUISIANA AND MISSISSIPPI AND THE FLOOD
PLAINS DRIED. THAT'S WHEN PANIC SET IN.

THE BLUE AND THE BLACK--THEY SAW
HUMANITY'S WASTEFULNESS AS AN
ACT OF WAR AGAINST THE WORLD.

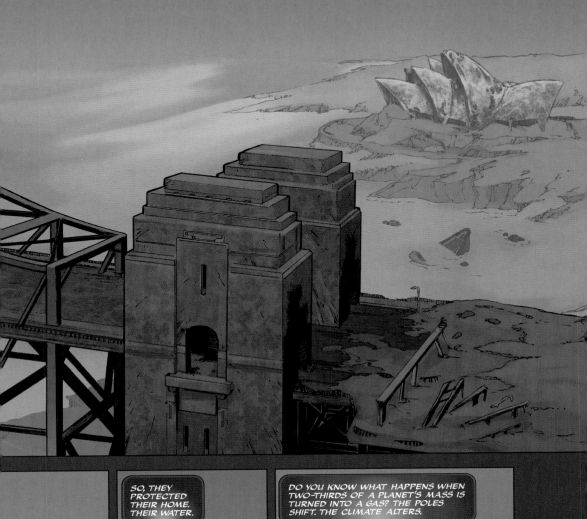

SO, THEY PROTECTED THEIR HOME. THEIR WATER.

AND ERADICATED THE REST.

DO YOU KNOW WHAT HAPPENS WHEN TWO-THIRDS OF A PLANET'S MASS IS TURNED INTO A GAS? THE POLES SHIFT. THE CLIMATE ALTERS.

PLANT LIFE? ANIMAL LIFE? DAMN NEAR *EVERYTHING* DIES.

ASPEN UNIVERSE REVELATIONS

CHAPTER
ONE

DIRECT EDITION COVER A TO
ASPEN UNIVERSE REVELATIONS #1
BY
JORDAN **GUNDERSON** | PETER **STEIGERWALD**

DON'T WORRY, GUYS...

THEN I'D BETTER GET MOVING.

HERE. IN CASE YOU NEED HELP. THEY'RE *MECHANICAL SCOUTS.*

...I'LL BE RIGHT BACK.

NNNNNNNN...!

PILI, YOU OKAY?

WHAT HAPPENED? YOU SEE SOMETHING? ANOTHER VISION?

NO...

...I DON'T SEE...

...ANYTHING.

TIME WAS, I THOUGHT I WAS JUST SOME KID. AN ORPHAN WITHOUT A CARE OR A PURPOSE.

BUT THE TRUTH IS--I'M KIND OF THE BATTERY FOR MAGIC IN THE WORLD. THE LATEST MANIFESTATION OF AN ETERNAL SPIRIT THAT HAS EXISTED SINCE THE DAWN OF TIME.

COMING AND GOING.

LIVING AND DYING.

ME, BUT NOT ME. NOT REALLY. MY SOUL. REINCARNATED. WHATEVER THAT MEANS.

AND NOW, THIS ME IS RIDING A MECHANICAL DRAGON THROUGH THE GOOEY CENTER OF THE UNIVERSE.

EAT YOUR HEART OUT, PREVIOUS ME'S.

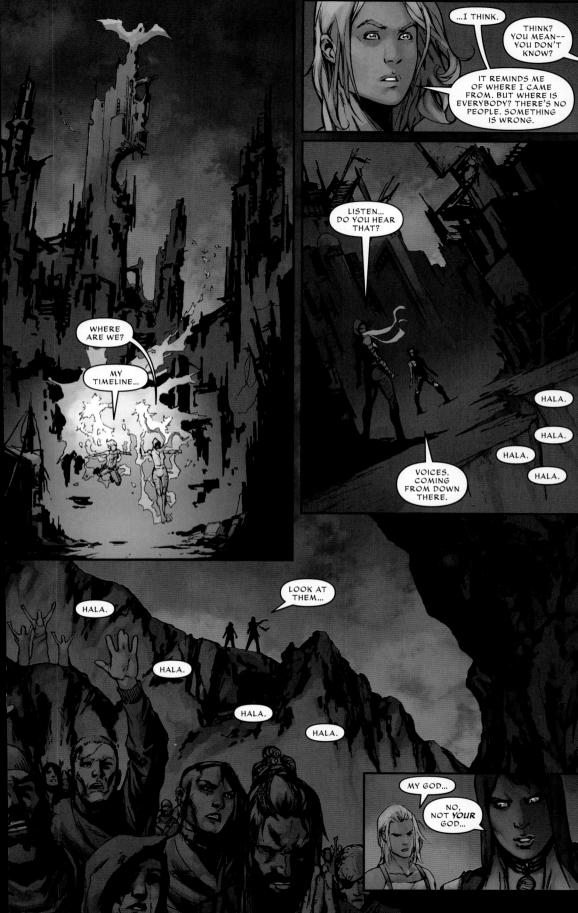

ASPEN UNIVERSE
REVELATIONS

CHAPTER
TWO

DIRECT EDITION COVER A TO
ASPEN UNIVERSE REVELATIONS #2
BY
Jordan **GUNDERSON** | Peter **STEIGERWALD**

MALIKAI!

HALAZEEL. ARE YOU INJURED?

I...DON'T KNOW. FEEL SO WEAK.

DID HE TRY TO STEAL YOUR MAGIC INSTEAD?

NO. THIS WAS SOMETHING ELSE.

WE MUST GO, NOW.

CAN YOU STAND?

I THINK SO.

WHAT HAPPENED?

HALAZEEL IS LIKE ME. HE HAS A UNIQUE CONNECTION TO THE MAGIC.

GUESS OUR SPIRITS SHORTED EACH OTHER OUT.

WELL, REGARDLESS--

YOU GOT HIM ON THE RUN. HEADING TOWARD WHO KNOWS WHERE.

IF YOU RECOGNIZED HIM WHEN YOU SAW HIM, ASPEN, THEN I'D SAY IT'S NOT A WHERE--

YES...

...I'M HERE.

WE MUST TAKE OUR LEAVE. IS THE MACHINE READY?

I BELIEVE SO, HALAZEEL. BUT THAT IS THE TRICKY PART ABOUT TIME MACHINES.

THE ONLY WAY TO KNOW FOR SURE IS TO TURN IT ON.

FOR TOO LONG, I HAVE RELIED ON TECHNOLOGY. IT HAS INFECTED EACH AND EVERY ASPECT OF MY EXISTENCE. IRONIC THAT NOW IT MAY PROVE TO BE MY WAY TO ESCAPE IT.

TO REGAIN A CONNECTION TO HUMANITY AND ALL THE MAGIC IT PROVIDES.

ASPEN UNIVERSE REVELATIONS

CHAPTER
THREE

Direct Edition Cover A to
ASPEN UNIVERSE REVELATIONS #3
BY
Jordan GUNDERSON | Peter STEIGERWALD

THIS IS MY WORLD.

I GREW UP LIKE EVERYONE ELSE. LIVED MY LIFE IN SAN DIEGO.

WENT TO SCHOOL. STUDIED. SWAM. A LOT.

ALWAYS FELT AT HOME IN THE WATER. GUESS THAT SHOULD HAVE BEEN MY FIRST CLUE.

TURNS OUT THAT UNDERNEATH IT ALL THERE WAS SOMETHING ELSE--SOMETHING MORE.

THE BLUE LIVED AND EVOLVED ON THE OCEAN FLOOR BEFORE HUMANITY CAME TO POWER. SURVIVED AND THRIVED.

AND ME? I BELONGED TO BOTH THE WORLD ABOVE AND THE WORLD BELOW.

WE'RE TOO LATE.

FOR SOME, BUT NOT ALL.

READY?

READY.

DEFINITELY MORE EFFECTIVE THAN SAVING FOLKS ONE AT A TIME.

STILL-- BETTER THAN NOTHING.

KILLIAN!

I HAD EVERYTHING UNDER CONTROL.

IF STARTING A WAR IS CONSIDERED UNDER CONTROL.

THEY ATTACKED US FIRST.

SURE. BECAUSE THANKS TO THAT MANIAC THEY THOUGHT WE WERE RESPONSIBLE FOR ALL OF THIS.

THEY ALWAYS BLAME US. FOR EVERYTHING.

THEY'RE GETTING BETTER.

NNNNN...

I'VE LOST... I'VE LOST IT ALL.

THEIR CHAOS IS OUR ORDER.

KABOOOM!!

PLEASE DON'T PUT US IN THE SAME GROUP. WE'RE NOTHING ALIKE.

ASPEN WAS RIGHT. HE'S TRYING TO INFLICT AS MUCH DAMAGE AS POSSIBLE.

NOW, I KNOW YOU DON'T BELIEVE THAT.

MAYBE I CAN DRAW HIM AWAY SO HIS AGGRESSION WILL ONLY COME AT ME. LET THE PEOPLE GET TO A SAFE PLACE.

IF THAT EVEN EXISTS ANYMORE.

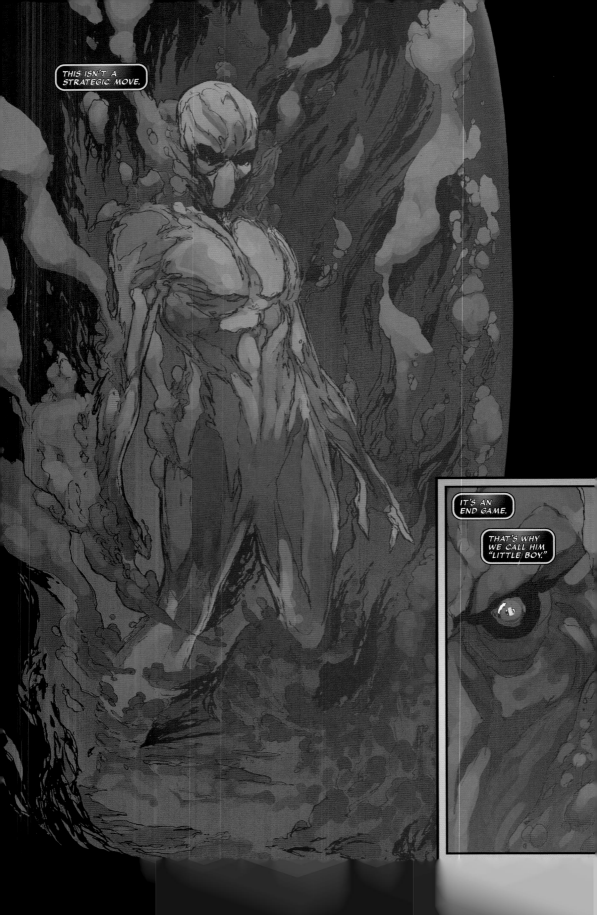

ASPEN UNIVERSE
REVELATIONS

CHAPTER
FOUR

FINE, I'LL DO IT ALONE.

IF HALAZEEL AND I SHARE THE SAME SOUL, THEN ALL I NEED TO DO IS FIND THE REST OF MYSELF.

NO ONE UNDERSTANDS WHAT IS COMING. THEY CANNOT SEE FAR ENOUGH DOWN THIS PATH WE ARE ON.
BUT, I DO. AND I WON'T LET THEM DESTROY EVERYTHING.
IF THEY WON'T ACCEPT THE BALANCE BETWEEN THE WORLD ABOVE AND THE ONE BELOW, THEN I WILL REMOVE THEIR CHOICE.
HALAZEEL WILL BE STOPPED. WITHOUT HIM, EVERYTHING WILL RETURN TO NORMAL. MY FRIENDS WILL BE ALIVE AND NOT WEIRDO EVIL VERSIONS OF THEMSELVES.
I WILL FIND HIM, AND I WILL END HIM, BECAUSE IF I DON'T, THEN EVERYTHING I LOVE WILL DIE.

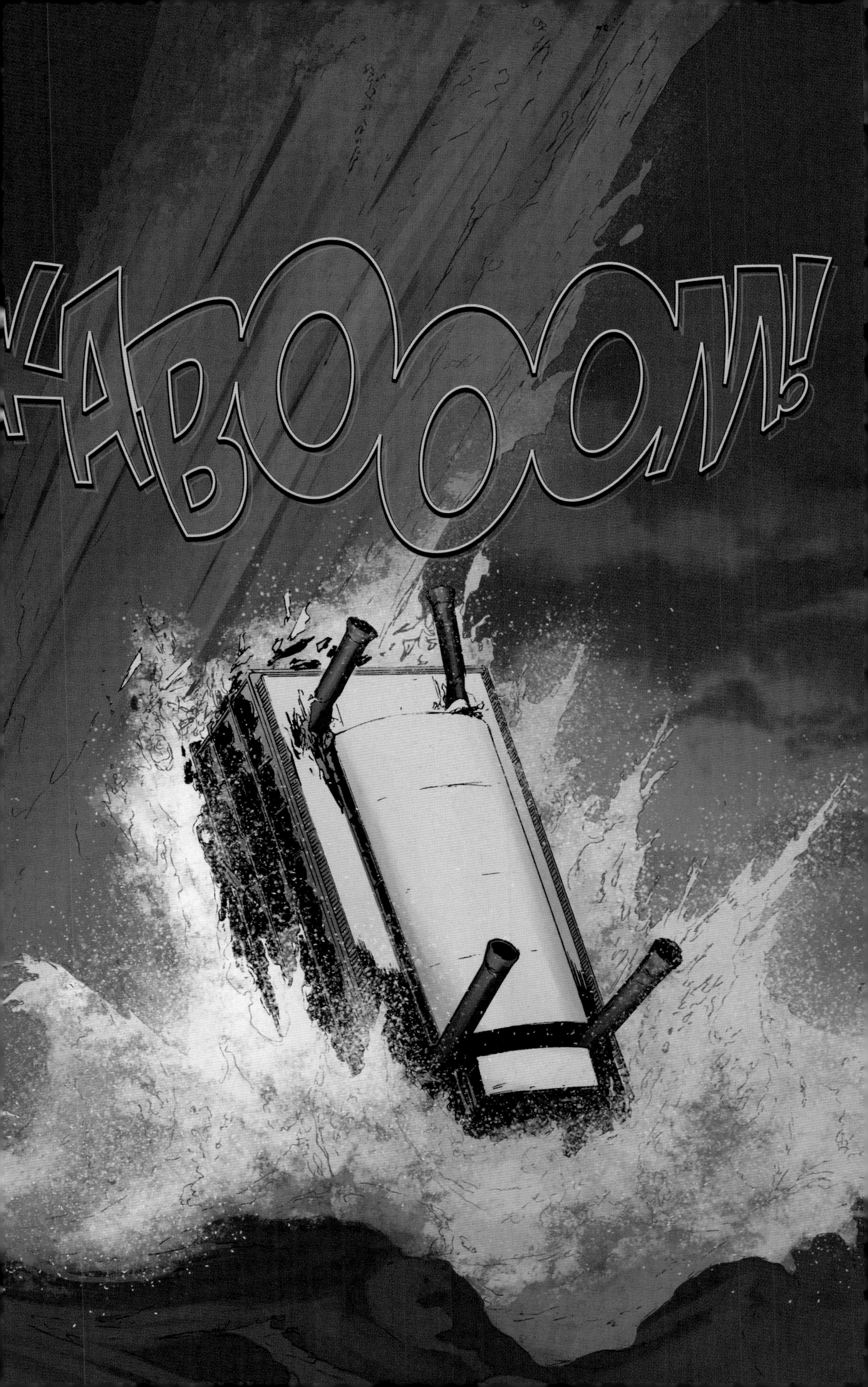
ABOOOM!

DESTROY IT ALL! WIPE THEM FROM THE EARTH!

WE WILL REIGN SUPREME AGAIN--

SPLORSH

-OOF!-

YOU DAMN FOOL.

I'M THE FOOL? YOU'RE THE ONE WHO HAD THE CHANCE TO ENSURE OUR VICTORY.

INSTEAD, YOU CLUTCHED AT SOME FANTASY THAT THE BLUE AND HUMANS COULD CO-EXIST.

WELL, LOOK AROUND, ASPEN. I TOLD YOU THIS WAR WAS INEVITABLE.

DAMMIT, KILLIAN. THERE ARE NO SIDES THIS TIME. THIS WILL BE THE END OF US ALL.

AS LONG AS IT ENDS THE HUMANS...

NO. I WILL NOT...WATCH...MY... WORLD...DIE...

NO... MORE...

THIS IS IT.

THE DOOMSDAY DEVICE THAT CHANGES EVERYTHING.

THE CATALYST FOR ARMAGEDDON.

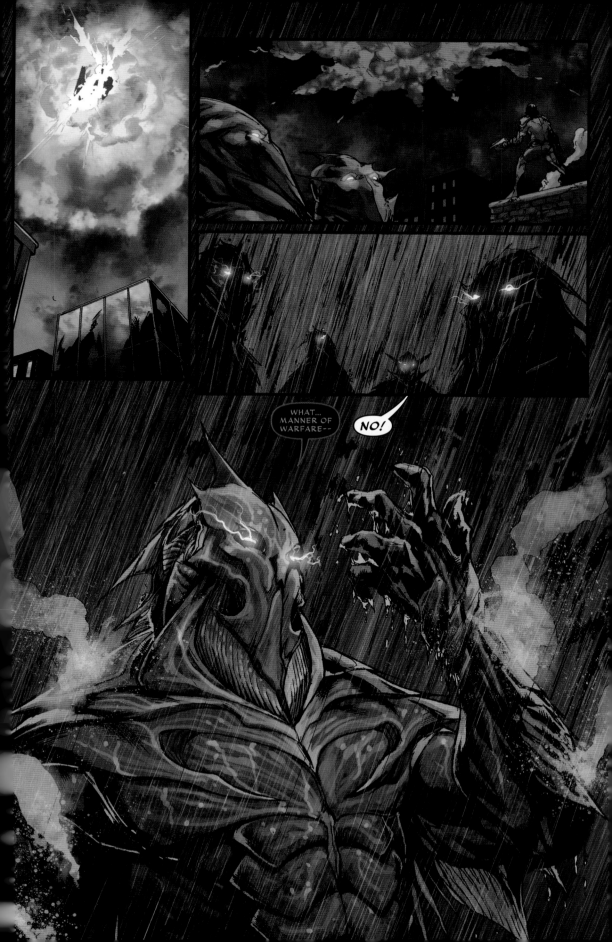

ASPEN UNIVERSE
REVELATIONS

CHAPTER
FIVE

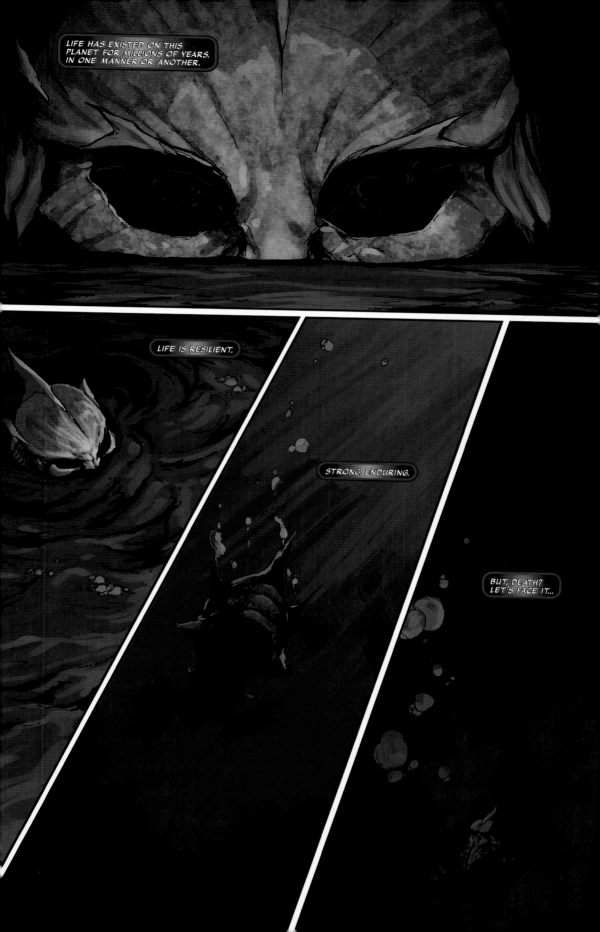

CHOOOM

THERE, THAT POWER SURGE LOOKS LIKE MAGIC TO ME.

I'M NOT GIVING UP. I CAN'T.

I WON'T.

MALIKAI!

TOO LITTLE, TOO LATE.

BUT THEN AGAIN, YOU MUST BE USED TO THAT, YES?

NO NEED TO SHED ANY TEARS.

YOU FORGET. ME AND THE BOY ARE ONE IN THE SAME.

YOU ARE NOTHING LIKE HIM.

GOT ROOM FOR ONE MORE?

STAY BACK!

BEAUTIFUL THING, ISN'T IT?

I COULD LISTEN TO THOSE WAVES ALL NIGHT. THE OCEAN IS SO PEACEFUL. DON'T YOU THINK?

SOMETIMES.

YOU COLD?

UH, YEAH.

FETCH ME MY SWEATER?

SURE.

BUT, MAYBE NEXT TIME DON'T USE THE WORD "FETCH." A GUY HAS HIS PRIDE.

OH CHANCE, I'LL REMEMBER THAT.

I KNOW YOU'RE OUT THERE. SHOW YOURSELF.

OVER HERE, BOY!

BOY? WHO YOU CALLING BOY, ONYX?

IF THE SHOE FITS.

THE VERY TINY SHOE.

YOU KNOW, RANIER, I THINK SHE IS WARMING UP TO ME. WHAT DO YOU THINK?

I THINK THAT I DO NOT CARE.

AND NEITHER SHOULD YOU.

DIRECT EDITION COVER C TO
ASPEN UNIVERSE REVELATIONS #1
BY
PAOLO **PANTALENA** | PETER **STEIGERWALD**

RETAILER INCENTIVE EDITION COVER D TO
ASPEN UNIVERSE REVELATIONS #1
BY
SIYA **OUM**

RETAILER INCENTIVE LIMITED EDITION COVER E TO
ASPEN UNIVERSE REVELATIONS #1
BY
Tyler **KIRKHAM** | Peter **STEIGERWALD**

COMIC-CON INTERNATIONAL SAN DIEGO 2016 EXCLUSIVE LIMITED EDITION COVER F TO
ASPEN UNIVERSE REVELATIONS #1
BY
ERIC **BASALDUA** | MARK **ROSLAN** | PETER **STEIGERWALD**

COMIC-CON INTERNATIONAL: SAN DIEGO 2016 EXCLUSIVE ASPEN CENTURY EDITION COVER H TO
ASPEN UNIVERSE REVELATIONS #1
BY
MICHAEL **TURNER** | MARK **ROSLAN** | PETER **STEIGERWALD**

AspenStore.com Customer Appreciation Exclusive Limited Edition Cover J to
ASPEN UNIVERSE REVELATIONS #1
BY
Michael **TURNER** | Mark **ROSLAN** | Peter **STEIGERWALD**

DIRECT EDITION COVER B TO
ASPEN UNIVERSE REVELATIONS #2
BY
PETER STEIGERWALD

DIRECT EDITION COVER C TO
ASPEN UNIVERSE REVELATIONS #2
BY
ALEX KONAT | MARK ROSLAN | PETER STEIGERWALD

RETAILER INCENTIVE EDITION COVER D TO
ASPEN UNIVERSE REVELATIONS #2
BY
TALENT **CALDWELL** | PETER **STEIGERWALD**

AFTER
AND FOR
MICHAEL

DIRECT EDITION COVER C TO
ASPEN UNIVERSE REVELATIONS #3
BY
GIUSEPPE **CAFARO** | MARK **ROSLAN** | PETER **STEIGERWALD**

AspenStore.com Black Friday Exclusive Cover D to
ASPEN UNIVERSE REVELATIONS #4
BY
JIM **LEE** | MARK **ROSLAN** | PETER **STEIGERWALD**